SUSAN GATES

The CLOWNS Next Door

Illustrated by
Bill Piggins

OXFORD
UNIVERSITY PRESS

OXFORD
UNIVERSITY PRESS

Great Clarendon Street, Oxford OX2 6DP

Oxford University Press is a department of the University of Oxford.
It furthers the University's objective of excellence in research, scholarship,
and education by publishing worldwide in

Oxford New York

Athens Auckland Bangkok Bogotá Buenos Aires Calcutta
Cape Town Chennai Dar es Salaam Delhi Florence Hong Kong Istanbul
Karachi Kuala Lumpur Madrid Melbourne Mexico City Mumbai
Nairobi Paris São Paulo Shanghai Singapore Taipei Tokyo Toronto Warsaw

and associated companies in Berlin Ibadan

Oxford is a trade mark of Oxford University Press
in the UK and in certain other countries

British Library Cataloguing in Publication Data
Data available

ISBN 0 19 917421 0

Printed in Hong Kong

Available in packs

Year 3 / Primary 4 Pack of Six (one of each book)   ISBN 0 19 917427 X
Year 3 / Primary 4 Class Pack (six of each book)   ISBN 0 19 917428 8

Contents

Chapter One

A family of clowns moved in next door. There was Mrs Clown, Mr Clown and Boy Clown. They all had white faces and red noses. They all wore baggy trousers and long, flappy clown shoes.

I was really excited. I spied on them from my bedroom window. I thought, "I bet clown families have loads of fun!"

But they didn't have much fun at all!

One afternoon I watched Mr Clown and Boy Clown come out of the house. They were carrying buckets of soapy water.

"This will be good," I told myself. "I bet they're going to have a big water fight!"

But they didn't throw sparkly jets of water at each other. They threw it over their car instead! Then they washed their car and dried it and polished it. I was really disappointed. I thought, "That's not very funny."

It wasn't even a clown car. The doors didn't fall off and it didn't have a horn that went, *"Parp, parp!"* It was just an ordinary car, like ours. It wasn't funny at all.

Then I saw Mrs Clown come out. She was carrying a plate of custard pies. I got excited all over again. "This is better!" I decided. "They're going to have a custard pie fight!

They're going to squish them in each other's faces."

I got ready for some big belly laughs, *"Ho, ho, ho!"*

But I didn't *"Ho ho ho."* I didn't even *"Tee hee hee."* Because Mrs Clown *handed* Mr Clown and Boy Clown a custard pie each. She didn't even throw them!

I nearly yelled out of the window, "What's funny about that?"

Next, I saw Mrs Clown come out with a big basket of washing. I thought, "This is more like it! She's going to hang some frilly knickers on the line! Silly, frilly, pink knickers, big enough to fit an elephant!"

But I was really disappointed. Their washing wasn't silly at all. It was ordinary, boring washing, just the same as ours.

I asked myself, "What's going on?" It was a mystery. Those clowns didn't do funny walks or chase each other or slip on banana skins. They didn't have a car that fell to bits. They didn't have funny washing. They didn't even *smile*. They just walked around looking miserable with their long clown's shoes going flap, flap, flap on the pavement.

I couldn't understand it at all. I thought, "Why are they dressed up like clowns when they don't do anything funny?"

Chapter Two

The next day I saw Boy Clown in the street. He was trying to juggle with tomatoes. But he kept dropping them. I thought, "He can't even juggle. All clowns can juggle!"

Splat! He dropped another tomato. This time it made a sticky red mess on his long, clown shoe.

I was disgusted. I decided, "That clown family are big cheats! They

wear clown costumes. But I don't
think they're *real* clowns at all."

I went up to Boy Clown. "If
you're a *real* clown, make me
laugh," I demanded.

He whisked a bunch of paper
flowers from up his sleeve.

"I'm not laughing," I told him.

He made his spotty bow tie twirl round. Then he made it light up like a Christmas tree.

"I'm still not laughing," I warned him.

"I'm trying my best!" said Boy Clown, looking really glum.

"Tell me a joke then!" I suggested. "Any joke will do. As long as it makes me laugh."

"I don't know any jokes," admitted Boy Clown, shaking his head miserably.

I'd never heard anything like it! A clown who doesn't know any jokes? I thought, "This is getting stranger and stranger!"

I gave him one last chance. "What's your name?" I asked him.

"Ryan," he told me.

"What, not Coco or Custard or Mr Chuckles? Ryan isn't a funny name. All clowns are supposed to have funny names! You're not really a clown at all, are you?"

"No," he confessed, looking a bit ashamed. "We're not real clowns. We're not very good at being funny, are we?"

"You're telling me! I could do a

better job myself! Which circus do you work for?"

"We got the sack from the circus," said Ryan, "because we couldn't make anyone laugh. The audience hated us. They booed and threw things. They shouted, 'Get off!' They shouted, 'Give us our money back!'"

"So why don't you stop being clowns?" I asked him. "I would, if I was as bad at it as you are."

"I wish we could," sighed Ryan. "It's awful, being clowns who aren't funny. But we can't stop. We can never, ever stop being clowns. We're stuck with it, for the rest of our lives."

"Why?" I asked him. This clown family was getting more and more mysterious! I was puzzled all over again.

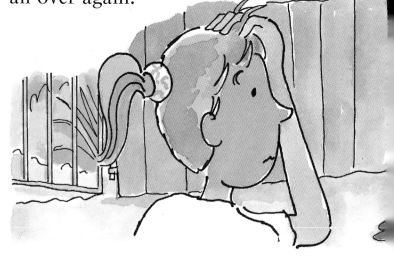

But he only said, "I musn't tell you. I'm not allowed. It's a terrible, terrible secret."

Then he went clumping off, his long clown's shoes slapping on the pavement.

Chapter Three

I just couldn't keep it to myself. I
told all the children in my street,
"That clown family has got a
terrible, terrible secret."

"What is it?" we asked each other.

We tried to guess. But we didn't
have a clue. So, one day, I suggested
we find out.

After tea, a gang of us crept up to

the clown house. Their garden was
like a jungle. It was spooky, full of
black, trembling shadows. Big trees
moaned in the wind. Their dark
branches poked at us like witches'
fingers.

"Ow, what's that?" I cried. Something had grabbed my ankle! I looked down. But it was only a thorny bramble stem.

"I'm scared," whispered the smallest boy. "I don't like it here."

I was scared too. I kept looking over my shoulder. Every time a tree branch creaked, I jumped.

We crouched down, right under their window.

"We shouldn't have come. Let's go home!" someone hissed.

"Shhh!" Very carefully, I peered into the house. I saw Ryan and his mum and dad sitting on the sofa. I felt really sorry for them. They looked so tired and fed up. They were taking off their clown make-up.

I thought, "We shouldn't be spying on them like this." But I was too curious to stop.

Mr Clown took off his frizzy, bright green, exploding hair. Mrs Clown cleaned off her white face. Ryan took off his red nose and his twirly bow tie.

A girl tugged at my arm. "Can you see anything?"

"Nothing interesting," I answered.

Then Ryan bent down to unlace his long clown's shoe. He pulled his foot out. His foot didn't stop. It kept coming and coming. It was never-ending!

"What can you see?" someone hissed at me again.

But I couldn't speak. I was too

shocked. All I could do was stare
and stare!

Ryan's mum was taking her shoes
off. Ryan's dad took his shoes off
too. They all had long, skinny,
flipper feet that fitted their clown's
shoes exactly!

I just couldn't help it. I cried out
in a really loud voice, "Yuk! Look at
that! How disgusting! They've got

horrible freaky feet! And they hide them inside their clowns' shoes!"

Three pairs of eyes swivelled round.

"They've seen me!" I thought, in a panic. They'd heard me be rude about their feet. They knew their secret had been discovered.

Ryan's mum rushed over to pull the curtains. We all jumped up.

"Run! Run!" I yelled.

We raced out of the shadowy garden, as if ghosts were after us.

Chapter Four

When I came home from school next afternoon, I went round to Ryan's house. I'd been thinking about Ryan and his mum and dad all day. I was sorry about lots of things. I wished I hadn't told everyone they had a secret or tried to find out what it was. Most of all, I wished I hadn't shouted rude things about their feet. I wanted to find Ryan and try to make friends.

But the clown family's car wasn't there.

I crept through their garden and looked in their windows. The rooms were all empty, except for one sad balloon and a bunch of crumpled paper flowers on the floor.

The clown family had moved away from our street. And it was all my fault.

Where were they? For months I couldn't stop worrying about them. Whenever a circus came to our area, I begged Mum, "Please take me!"

We went to every circus for miles around. I wasn't interested in the trapeze artists or the fire-eaters or the acrobats. I only waited for the clowns to come tumbling into the

ring. But it was never them. The
clowns we went to see were always
funny. They had proper clown cars
that fell to bits. They did funny

tricks. They made people laugh. No one shouted "Get off!" or, "Give us our money back!" So they couldn't be my clowns, the clowns who used to live next door.

I worried about Ryan and his mum and dad so much, I even had dreams about them. I dreamed they'd got another job in a circus. They were trying their hardest. Ryan was making his bow tie light up and twizzle at top speed! Mr Clown was putting treacle down his trousers. It should have been funny. But somehow, when he did it, it wasn't. Nobody laughed. Instead, the audience got more and more angry.

"Clear off!" they yelled. "You useless clowns!"

They chucked rotten eggs at them

and squishy tomatoes. The clown
family had to run out of the circus
ring. It was awful.

Ages passed. Summer turned into
winter, then back into summer
again. I never gave up looking or
worrying about them. But Ryan and
his mum and dad seemed to have
vanished off the face of the earth.

Chapter Five

Then, one day, my class went on a school trip to Sea World.

We walked through glass tunnels. Octopuses waved their tentacles at us. Sharks grinned as they swam overhead. Rays glided past us like flying carpets.

In the afternoon, our teacher said, "Now Class Three, we're having a special treat. We're going

WAY OUT

to see some dolphins."

As we took our seats round a big lagoon, I felt really excited. Beyond the lagoon was the deep blue sea.

A lady said over the loudspeaker, "Ladies and gentlemen, here come the dolphins!"

At first, I couldn't see anything. Then, far, far out at sea, I saw a silver rainbow flash in the sun. It leapt out of the waves. Then another rainbow flashed. Then another.

"Dolphins!" we all shouted.

They came streaking through the waves towards us. They were going to come really close, right inside the lagoon!

"Look, look," someone said. "There are people swimming with them."

"And here, leading the dolphins to see you," said the loudspeaker lady, "are Sea World's famous dolphin experts. This family were born to swim with dolphins. Dolphins are their best friends!"

I was hardly listening. I was just staring. *"Wow!"* That was all I could say, *"Wow!"*

It was Ryan and his mum and dad! But they had bathing suits on, not clown suits. They were as swift and graceful as dolphins in the water. And all because of those brilliant flipper feet!

I stood up to get a better view. Ryan's feet flickered. He went flying through the waves! His feet flickered again. He dived deep with the dolphins. Then twisted high in the

air with them. He looked really happy.

I thought, "What a show!"

"Hey, Ryan!" I waved and shouted. I thought, "Will he wave back? I wouldn't blame him if he didn't." But he did! He gave me a big, friendly wave.

At the end of the show, the audience stood up and clapped and cheered. No one yelled, "Get off!

You're useless!" Everyone shouted, "Hurrah! More! More!"

I shouted, "Hurrah!" louder than anyone. I had a huge grin all over my face.

I thought, "I can stop worrying about them now. They've found something they really like doing. They don't have to be clowns. They don't have to hide their flipper feet inside clown shoes any more."

Ryan and his mum and dad swam back out to sea with the dolphins. We all waved and cheered until they were just tiny dots in the distance.

About the author

I live in County Durham with my three children and I can remember the exact moment when I got the idea for this story. We were watching clowns on television and my son said, "Do those clowns' shoes *really* fit their feet?" Hey presto, *The Clowns Next Door* was born! Simple, wasn't it? But maybe the simplest ideas are the best.